A Deeper
Anthology

(Volume 1)

A Deeper *Anthology*

The Heart
The Soul
The Being

(Volume 1)

Created and Written by
Perry Douglas Sisk

CITIOFBOOKS, INC.
3736 Eubank NE Suite A1
Albuquerque, NM 87111-3579
www.citiofbooks.com
Hotline: 1 (877) 389-2759
Fax: 1 (505) 930-7244

Ordering Information:
Quantity Sales. Special discounts are available on quantity purchases by corporations, associations, and others. For details, contact the publisher at the address above.

Printed in the United States of America.

ISBN-13   Paperback   978-1-960952-98-1
                   eBook   978-1-960952-99-8

Library of Congress Control Number: 2023915290

Table Of Contents

Heart And Soul And Being
(July 12, 2001)

The Heart belongs and beats
for all
that have a voice in which to call
and echo down a hallowed hall
in absence to the heart we fall

the soul is captured by all that are born as
though is fragile a web that is torn
through life we love and yet may we scorn
A soul gone unseen and left so forlourne

Our being is our most treasured host
for in there we place with love and with most
surpassed by one and dare we will boast
for all that it holds in silence a ghost

This human spirit nurtured with drive
and keeping the flame and light so alive
for years of its length of labor to strive
an ocean so deep no man will yet dive

For in all of these things reside with one cost
just this one thing was found and not lost
this human heart with soul and of being
Mans Spirit God had created now seeing

A Mother's Love And Tears
(December 21, 2009)

When looked into a mother's eyes
and wonder wisdom there
cannot account for tears she cries
or heartache strife in life she bare

taking care to always give
to those she held and bore in pain
did this mothers wonder live
as long as there is rain

The breath she takes to bend the tide
and keep a love nonyielding
injustice she did take in stride
and yet with love was shielding

A mother's eyes can hold a grace
of such no one can know
with tear stain on her face
a Love for all does flow

This I saw in mothers eyes
a glance that I once viewed
a shaking head and heavy sighs
Passing on yet born again
in heaven she's renewed

In dedication to my mother - Joetta Irene Sewell, departed 17th of January 2011. Always held in memory.

A Chair I Share
(January 21, 2010)

Sittin' all alone in my easy chair
giving thought to issues and I don't care
never gonna ever want to go back there
them salad days of past years I had and seen
runnin' through a painted meadow filled with green
take a number wait in line and steal some time
find another love sublime
beyond the mountains high that few can climb
to stand alone amidst a crowd
or ride air currents and grasp a cloud
to soar up high and embrace the sky
the shinning stars and twinkled eye
We faulter still and lesser learn
where flame resides and always burn
to yield to feelings once were shared
and finding with who be paired
seek solution and strive to hold
no absolution leaves one cold
for in my chair of ease and peace is
this where life will end and cease
to calmly step apart from life
having known a measured strife
what will we learn in given time
for in these words do hold in rhyme
One Loves to share and always care
while sitting in my easy chair

A Depth To Share
(February 21, 2010)

A gift to share and be one's own
to have yet keep and be it known
If not for self tho on one shelf
for true you are as oceans blue
tho still not known or seen by few
while given time and sought by rhyme
one's deeper depth and held sublime
to give of self and less abstain
and harken to the falling rain
in seasons time throughout one year
and hopes to fall upon one's ear
some words we'll treasure and too will heed
as souls when scattered spirits freed
I often wonder shared with one
all to what end one day is done

A Heart That's Stolen
(December 18, 2009)

Giving wonder in reflections of, how passion
governs everlasting love
too seldom seen for its truer value or worth
to grasp that one initial breath an infant will at birth
In keeping narrow the path we tried and yet witness the
purity of the Dove

In all the fables ever told and all the favors ever Bold
All that's offered in life yet so often taken for naught
a most treasured attainment ever bought
Ones heart is rarer than any glittering Gold

Does he still hold your heart
and must you ever part
said to be captured from the start
will he always hold your heart

Timid are the ways of our early learning days
compassion for others being a sought after trait
Maturing faster disallow all our better ways
Seeking virtue in moderation at that Golden Gate

No words will deliver or encompass better meaning
Than ones truer Heart being filled of Joy and Love
Can one day know from mountains high and leaning
How high the blue will reach in all the skies above

Will he still Hold your heart
Tho know was stolen from the start
this walk thru life did drift apart
Held by one and always forever has your Heart

A Heart To Miss
(January 30, 2010)

To walk alone and stand apart and give
so freely from your heart
In dreams we cherish times gone by the
subtle glimmer in one's eye

Truer known and long for still
captured held against ones will
a freedom once took so for granted with
many seeds of deeds were planted

To taste the grapes of life its wine on
cloudy days the sun still shines
To look beyond and past ones faults
one Marching soldier sighs and haults

One thought to always seek will find
somewhere hidden deep in mind
For whom the many choose to follow
those souless few and oh so hollow

Be yet filled with spirits
Bold resist and weather bitter cold
In heated passions cause and storm does
take upon familiar form

So stand alone and feel the Heart Of
crowded halls yet set apart having
lived and been alone
who's walked beside and onward shown

Stood Not apart and never distant
Be those known and heaven sent
with hearts of angels wings of gold
So costly some not bought nor sold

A Heart Will Test The Time
(April 2, 2010)

What words are spoke in every song
To clue you in that I was wrong
The Seas and oceans Tides that bare
Are You the Same why did you care

We once and always knew from when
along and each our sides to spend
Devotion Worship bending time
My Heart for yours Was yours Yet Mine

From the west coast on and far across and
landing East as if to toss
a feeling shared and this I know With
Winter blankets White the snow

To always chase and calm your fear and
simple as my being near
To hold and cherish just this one
In time unending the years that run

In Words I voice to you alone as
carved or etched in every stone
along the hillsides valleys low
My love of you yet do you know

One Song that spoke of words that rhyme to
better test our love in time
This always true and always Known I'm
made for You and Time has shown

A Hidden Dream
(August 12, 2009)

I often find you at my side
then also see you run and hide
Why won't you hand around and see
Or are you just afraid of me
I offer nothing more of me
than all there is that you can see
Your Voice your touch is something rare
Why Can't you see that i do care
In dreams we walk and freely share
Each others thoughts with whispers there
Then waken to this vacancy
This space you filled tho yet did flee
I find you close and yet so far
As if to try and grasp a Star
One day i long for yours and mine
Our hearts and souls to intertwine
In only dreams you still abide
From there i see in You i hide

There once were seven people
who our nation barely knew
they each in turn did touch the sky
and fly where all is blue
they rode a chariot made of steel
and with their rockets blaze
setting off toward the sky
in awesome misty haze
though reaching high and short of grasp
the atmosphere had held
they broke the glass of heavens clasp
their ship though strong with weld

this seven valiant few now fly
in heavens lofty space
no longer kept beneath the sky
nor fight to win the race
their passage to blue limits blue
so named the challenger
now giving all eternal view
to mans futured calendar
so stars now named far into heaven
do hold this valiant 7

P douglas Sisk,,,,,24/feb/1987

Angles Hidden Task
(December 23, 2009)

Believe there are angels amidst our living
Seeking out to those apart
Always be they Faint of heart
These Angels noticed for their giving

In taken long with winds across
Have yet to dawn their wings
and still are separate from all beings
Consider more for them who's Loss

In view if evidence they be true
once and always found in trust
In many crowed halls too few
Departed from returned from dust

Given faith from heavens door
and chart their course thru humanity
Lending hands to helpless poor
and still yet spare their vanity

In all we hear one call and becon still
these angels seen as common people
In charge of tasks with deeds of will
their wings bestowed
A church its steeple

A Breeze Of Change
(March 16, 2010)

while subtle breeze gather leaves around my feet
I wonder and gaze at kids at play across my street
knowing in my youth I had done the same
pickin and choosin who in the game

Life itself has become one tried and true
tho often leaving so many so blue
as fall a season to ready natures slumber
and still with clouds that rumble of thunder

is often yielded to calmer dawns
as chess is made surrender the pawns
tho looking past and seeing beyond
how still the water upon a pond

being told of legends and myth
just who I belong and who to walk with
this journey in life of solitude and peace
I still would want this silence to cease

when found of one and know for sure n certainty
has it come to pass out of only purity
did fate alone deliver a change for some
to allow a better purpose to come

these ponderments I have when gazing at my feet
and notice the ways of folks who cheat
as those kids at play that say your it
as this breeze of change delivers me as I sit

Chased Dreams
(December 21, 2009)

Men chasing dreams from where will find
those best discovered apart from his past
when in time Men seek tho blind
awaken still with hopes that last

Men given abilities far and above
all too often fail to share
as with pure the snow and white the dove
in slumber essence where giving care

Mans reach for things not meant to be
in all creation and time past moments
Why yet in all pursuits we see
Fail and drift as winds with torrents

Man can achieve best well kept ambition
to all that may ponder with devotion
to ever witness true fruition
A passion depth surpass an ocean

Men Hold to dreams a driving force
Holding candles flame to seek
standing fast to one chartered course
thoughts shared from others often speak

Thus in keeping charge of merrit and
standing firm and strong thru strife
tho times so painful just to bare it
Mans dreams he chases on thru Life

Counted Chances
(December 20, 2009)

Life is said be filled with chances
So searched for too with random glances
When looked upon from distant view
A life we live turns a different hue
an early morning sun that shines cross
dim horizons submits to loss
as seasons pass and years will becon
a measured fee, have cost one lesson
never doubting life renews
some as one and some by two's
embracing breath and longing for
continued on and long for more
One chance among so many given
and not forsake ones will thats driven
why ask a question no answers for
why blue the sky we do ignore
One's wisdom earned for having strength
to last the years and lifes full length
unanswered prayer tho in an end
was answered still where we begin
Time marches on and all will pass
into a realm where spirits last
are souls that gather among our living
sharing chances from those yet given
countless are those chances known

but seeing all as wind thats blown
looking back and amazed so still
while set upon a windowsill

Encompassed Trait
(December 13, 2009)

To walk a path we dare not follow
as bitter wine refuse to swallow
in each and varied courses taken
from dreams emersed why still awaken;
are lies we tell a twisted truth
as age with wisdom torments our youth
by lite of candle struggle see
the dawning day and darkness flee;
endowed few are of virtue trait
as many stand in line and wait
passioned love refuse to yield
this awesome power bar and shield;
Far in truth and measured test
endure a hardship longs for rest
tolerant passive patience known
are these rare qualities we've outgrown;
within the confines of our past
our path we choose yet can we last
for life most struggle getting through;
religions righteous holding firm
until one day we're asked we learn
in testament of our paths we traveled
some so smooth and more were graveled;

in seeking closure lust for finality
what payment made from our humanity
evaluated tested tried and true
one final goal that all attain
to witness all that which we knew

Fast Way Home
(January 19, 2010)

well I'm off and gone for a brandnew dawn never
lookin back and to a future im drawn
the tides are turnin and my wheels are burnin
just tryin to beat the mornin home

frigid winter cold are some hearts i have known
never havin tears for the fears they've never shown
seeking better wisdom for their hearts of stone
tryin to keep in sight of places they did rome

bittersweet at times is a memory we have shared
and knowin not a soul or a person that ever cared
still consider feelings of the many some we spared
shiny and clean as the polished chrome

when your tryin to beat the mornin sun
taken on those tasks better left undone
walk awhile and sigh then ya choose to run
just tryin to beat the dawning home

lookin back on times that were always filled with fun
keepin track of seeds of good deeds you had done
the best a father wishes to pass on to his son
just to try and beat all his mornins home

For A Dream Sake
(July 18, 2010)

Throughout and in our lifetime someone comes along
to make our sun shine brighter and be they right or wrong
For Some were steered into or past beyond their hopes
and others steadfast kept with passions bound in ropes
For me it seemed to come and go with ease
as tho the leaves of fall are tossed upon the breeze
To always hope and yearn for tear sake beckoned call
and always find ones Heart for my own to often fall
As years now pass so swiftly and still look far ahead
Why can i not look Back and see just where things were led
For one im always meant and bound for given time
With words of every song been written and cast into one ryhme
When called upon to prove or simply to reveal
This heart for you i've kept and you
who broke the seal
Now wonder in the meadows of green and somber shaded lane
As mountains valleys with their streams for
me along you came
One whispered promise gave to me and held
with high esteem
the chance id find for me and You
Tho hidden in one dream

Friend
(February 5, 1985)

As I sit in stillness still
my mind it wonders strong of will
Should I sleep and dream of peace
Shall I find my thoughts to cease

Should I wonder why my friend
You call yourself this to an end
What price was paid for efforts sake
in ones heart you placed a stake

For true is Love a friend so few
as numbered drops of morning dew
In trust of many yet hurt so long
So often seen my trust done wrong

I give and gave through years and spend
One helpful hand a friend to lend
and ask for pay they surely do
One friend in life my own I knew
Myself as you I still ask who
One friend to friend my one was YOU

The Heart, The Soul, The Being, The Human Spirit
(July 12, 2001)

The heart belongs and beats
to all
that have a voice by which to call
and echo down a hollowed Hall
in absence of the heart we fall
The Soul is captured of all thats born
as tho a fragile Web is torn
through life we love and yet do scorn
A soul unseen yet left forlourne
The being is our treasured host
For in there place with Love of most
surpassed by one we dare not boast
For in it holds one Silent ghost
The Human Spirit nutured drive
While keeping flame and light alive
For years their length and labor strive
With oceans depth too deep to dive
For in these things reside with cost
Just one thing was found not lost
This human heart with soul one Being
One Spirit GOD created Seeing

A Heart That Dreams
(March 18, 2010)

I dreamed a dream of one and I
as tho this one had fell from the sky
took my heart and breath away
yet knowing still not meant to stay
what gift I dreamed here once bestowed
this one had strength with eyes that glowed
in my own with awe and hope
yet felt once waken I could not cope
is said in things do hold one purpose
tho be for me to hold one curse
being close too far to reach
try counting grains upon a beach
this one for me my heart did steal
with mask in hand yet too reveal
when placed upon this ones true face
which gazed upon one tear a trace
I'm left with now so and bitter and true
this one that spoke I'm meant for who still
facing truth beyond all care
what fills the void left hidden there
Embrace a dream and long remain what
more to loose or less will gain
This one for me to never leave
and keep my mended hearts reprieve
while tho in slumber a heart is taken
down to the soul this one had shaken

Hearts Mending Ways
(September 24, 2010)

All things have one start one ending
for all the hugs and hearts some lending
in all when time goes on unbending
what signals real unreal most sending

We meet and greet and pass the moments
as watching seas of waves and torrents
Test of time and passion warrants
What makes small wonder ones observance

We offer all we ever thought true
Tho always seek from Who to who
One to bond with one thats few
Tho still in light of day no clue

Associations for some will pass
In most are yet familiar class
As lookin past and thru some
Glass We fail and fall into the Mass

So Many long for truth and trust yet
some removes the bread its crust
meet we some for Love or Lust
A driven Force with Force we must

So in all things that started ending The time
between goes on and bending Time it curves
and stretches sending
Back to One Love We Love With
Hearts So Mending

Hearts Of Fate
(December 23, 2009)

Was it unexpected that id find one true
how does destiny fall in the laps of so few
given time and said and done
who would haveknown you'd be my one

while searching seeking looking far
as while I look up to one star
Fate played to me a welcome plan
and placed you here so close at hand

In dreams I always sort of knew
my life so singular now into
One others heart did steal away
forever keeping and never stray

Time seems to drag on slow and long
as if words so repeated thru a song
Sad but true in thoughts of you
Dare I miss your messaged clue

Kept by faith and Hopes of late
with all roads narrow long and straight
Belong to one and one for always
with hearts so joined and ever stays

Loves Hidden Sprout
(January 5, 2010)

Aint it funny where seeds can sprout
all around and scattered about
but deep within a heart of gold
where seeds of Love are bought and sold

We look upon and seek to find
those seldom seen and yet so kind to
ponder visions where is kept
in slumbered embrace tho where had slept

Wake to find an empty space
and yet with silence in thoughts to chase
looking for one thing we lost
knowing Not for having cost

In truth and passion boundless shore
as vast an ocean and never more
to capture once or still again
One Seed still sprouted deep within

one tree of Love grow strong and tall
with limbs and branches thru every fall
Do often shed their leaves of green
A love so deep yet never seen

Tho one day found and treasured Long
as words are written created song
To hold to fast and stay a course
A power in Love an awesome force

For having seeds of Love where planted
into ones Soul yet unrecanted
Where still will grow and left alone
A seed yet sprouts beneath a stone

One Highway To Love
(January 12, 2010)

Headed out down those highways
lookin up toward them skyways
passin up all them byways
searchin for a love

Lookin past them tall trees
travel across them many seas
where upon bended knees
still searchin for my love

wonderin the time will take
and call it for heavens sake
would ya cause my world to shake
when I finally find my Love

when I finally find a Love
will it be sent from high above
elusive as a dove
takes me back down highways

yeh drivin out down highways
and climbin up long stairways
Ii had nothing to lose noways
tryin to capture love

tryin to capture love elusive as a dove
and angel fell from above
in the middle of my highway

throw caution against the wind
only one I want to spend
times left I have to lend
One Love down my Highway

Land Or Water Origin Be
(December 22, 2009)

While looking on still waters still
with ever present calm and depth
a lake or river that rains do fill
with banks holding back as if a breath

the oceans tide sweeps far and wide
with sandy beaches fall upon
giving waves such ease and stride
yet falls so silent with each new dawn

few men will know or even heed
what miracles made from where and too
did all life stem from just one seed
divine intervention paints the sea its blue

evolutions claim from water were born
and tho yet still others will attest
theres one truer fabric from which were torn
Thus be Gods children in faith is best

For how in number many faces be
when looked upon for all things worth
and miracle dismissed so casually
evolution or creation men still given birth
Born of water OR of earth

Love In Time
(May 24, 2001)

When in time and when to change
So vast in Love to all seem strange
Encumbered souls with depth to feel
As far across a ranchers range;
To few that know of life one gift
A passion high as high can lift
As tides that surge upon the Shore
The desert sands of time will sift;
Through all that heaven holds within
Do pictures hold yet capture then
As hearts unfold and yielding truth
How full with burden all that sin;
One issue here and be it clear
One love so far and still so near
From words that march in candid Rhyme
No others know their one true fear;
One Love to hold
To love in Time

Once in life there comes a time to know
one love so profound and yet so rare,
While knowing we can never share,
for the undying certainty it held.
Be we bound by laws of conscience and
moral simplicities, this Love I speak of
Held for me.

For me it held a passage, a passage no
Oceans depth could reach, of passion and security
of mind, body and soul did this Bond hold
With one so far from reach and yet so near

I dared to touch in meager steps while
yet well knowing the end result.
In this life so few are days to look upon
with dampened eyes and yet tho struggle
Keep them dry,
We go on to see what cards are dealt
for reality does speak the mind while
yet all else does touch the heart
So bitter sweet with pain severe
it touches the heart so near
Once held for sake of wisdom there yet
yielding to one valid truth, I knew in
time that passed me by,that once I did
have wings to fly, For in that bond i held

with One, a truer Soul connected once
tho left untold through strife of life
and lust for love of life itself.

I Ponder now why cross my path if
not to teach a lesson there,
this one true fact that I have found
and keep so treasured utter sound
being NOT subject to interpretation,
In view of knowin what life did offer
I know now more of what was given,
Why I chose not to take is better left
to mystery, for in all things reside
two sides, when one is left alone and without
mutual thought of being, the two cannot
exist in union

YET still apart A Bond is there
One bond so strong that time won't share
Could this all be led by fate,
Was it left as destined Late
I guess the answer lies with all things kept
With this one Love so deep and yet
in Step
In dreams I see few moments held
as tho on film with passions weld
Should there come to me a reason.
Searched for yet missed with every season
An answer to one question seek
Why did GOD create the meek?

To be given chance to have but never hold
What all would keep as sacred Gold
This one true Love I could not grasp
but tasted of and wish would last
Words will never show this true devotion.

LOVES UNCERTAINTY
(May 21, 2001)

never attained by any measure of courage
or faith
One Love surpassed all descriptive analogies
and I suppose the why's are less important
Now what I see is this spirit lost, detached
from a soul a Love it cost
Not noticed for its worth and left unvalued
by the one
I alone now understand for in my capacities
where treasures of this heart abide
I am aware of burdens there
Many have been so cautiously kept
While Time has healed those scars not shown
now only one is close at hand to cover
all previous wounds were sewn
So near to fracture now its state, and when it's broken
beyond repair and know I will Rate
Through troubled stillness Grief comes
to lend a tearing eye
By way of exhausted feelings now having
been allowed to grow, to encompass
just one more certain love I know
As years will add in number Still
in itself gives cause to yield
One loss of love this Heart has known

As cold the bitter winter shown
I Leave this stage of life and go on
To what is sure to be
Just one more LOVES UNCERTAINTY

Love Spilled Upon One Windowsill
(December 30, 2009)

When you place your heart upon a windowsill
and Gaze out upon true natures lawn
and taking in so much at will
to see the dew that wets a dawn

I know your standing there to cast
in light and shadow of your past
to go beyond and to outlast
and stand alone and standing fast

For voices given speaking Not
Do hearts so rule or guide in thought
for giving favor and be for naught
So many lessons yet be they taught

You've placed your heart upon a Sil
Be strong of passion and wonder still
To offer one and only One
Your deepest Love an unborn Son

A Heart so filled with room for more
and all this Life do keep in place
Where has been told in keeping score
and in full measure wins the race

A Chase to understand and why in wrath
with ones true Heart and beating still
a long and narrow highways path
Was your heart the one did spill

Measure Of Depth
(December 08, 2009)

Yesterday we shared a past,
Tomorrow what will last
Looking on and Looking Back
To view those things we Lack
In time to collect Tho loosing Fast
In you i see the all of me
In Me is seen in part is you
When two are one and all is done
is there yet in keeping One
Is said that Love has endless ties
But what of all the endless Skies
Are Stars a measure of our souls
As far and long a River Flows
Timid Meek and Passive Pride
In me so Much does hide
While longing for a better stride
Oceans Deep and endless tide
Herein my spirit forever abide

A Missin' Situation
(May 29, 2010)

Why is it a hittin missin situation
with some kissin on occassion
just to want for some relaxation
from this missin situation

we met with better provocation
and we had the motivation
to spend some hours communication
what had sparked our declaration

But this hit n missin situation
leaves me more infatuation
but surpasses indignations
yet still I miss this situation

were you sent from constellations
with stars beyond imagination
in my life you make foundation
yet i need your situation

So on with missin situations
as long as kissin more on all occassions
we'll share our all in relaxations
we never missed this situation

My Fathers Handed Gift
(December 11, 2009)

I once held to thinkin I'd shake My fathers Hand
Before He was taken to walk on heavens Sand
As a child of ten or so I was always into things
Dad would chase the bee's away taking all their stings
He watched out for me although my youth could not allow
the fact I was his gift that God for him endow
As I grew into a Man of lesser early years
I always seen the heartache I caused in Daddy's tears
Lookin back and wishin now I coulda been a better Son
who was better off after all was said and done
I often close my eyes and dream of better days
and try and recall my Dad his patient better ways
Taken from me sooner than I was ready for
Dad was made to enter quickly that golden heavens door
As for now the years passing quickly I come to realize
those days he looked at me with loving calming eyes
I kind of took for granted he would always be around
But in his passing on did leave a shaking ground
I always held to feel that I could shake the hand
Of the man My Dad he would see my wedding band
As I grew on to manhood and took my wife he'd see
now in my heart I'll treasure all he meant to me
I miss my fathers voice tho at times I often hear
He tells me he is proud and i sence that he is near
Though he left me in all to brief a time
These words I've written here, his gift to me in rhyme

My Children (For Alice)
(March 18, 2010)

No Limited Cost
(May 21, 1983)

As we have gazed upon our creation
Is there still doubt as to limitation
Why do we strive on earth yet to be
Knowin how vast all that we see
Abundance of all this world has to give
Seldom tho cry when ceasing to live
Allowing for Mans long struggle to reign
For his was to take nor less any Pain
Her Loss was said to be solely our gain
What are we all now with cause for refrain
Her Surface Now bare with sky as unblue
Her fruits she once bore no more to renew
Restoring a truth and hold to a trust
Yet Man he still takes as tho he just must
With thoughts to reflect as seasons now gone
What choice will we have when left all alone
No birds left to sing or doves that would fly
No rivers long running reflecting a Sky
Should Man move on to worlds yet unknown
What will Man have learned to atone
This world we have known created hereof
When allowed to depart beyond and above
Will Man ever be given a one second chance
For all that's been seen He seen with one glance
Created this world with time so unclear
Another perhaps and Yet will we fear
For all Man has made may yet be his loss
How will he then measure
No Limited Cost

Old Farm Raisin
(December 12, 2009)

Once Held
(June 6, 2001)

Often searched for countless days
Those endless thoughts and timeless ways
To find few words that speak so much
Though Words do fall beneath one Touch

In all this world and all creation
Throughout this spance and past duration
Does love surpass its own extinction
Tho brought to life through self distinction

Viewed by many with boundless meaning
Fear to shatter as crystal leaning
Held in our grasp though never known
Blind to its light and never shown

Yet still we find that once was told
For in all hearts One constant Weld
All too few and many Bold
This indignation Hearts
Once Held

One Beaten Heart
(July 25, 2010)

How many times does a heart
need to hurt
before you come to
realize your gonna loose your shirt
How many times does your heart
have to heal and mend
and come to see all the strife it all will lend
Were it not for Fate and chance that
we all just like to dance yet struggle
just to try so hard when taken by one glance
given to the meek this earth eternal
do angels earn their wings
and still hide them proudfully
This heart of mine been given Full
and often eagerly
Just to end up on the ground
walked on beaten down and hurt repeatedly
Still ready for another round it seems
to hold for someone new
with scars to show as seams
yet truely known by few
A heart can not be known
by who it holds so dear
but better kept for all its worth
by others it will fear

Still keep its passion near

One Higher Sound
(December 11, 2009)

Seen an eagle in the sky one day
Didn't know if lost or at play
he soared in circles and high aloft
serene his flight with feathers soft
then walk along a stream i see
Looking down at fish that flee
always swimming fast with ease
as if to taunt and want to tease
Then and too along forrest edge
a Grizzly bear along rocks wedged
Did turn with eyes and piercing glare
stood i still unmoving there
As nature all this world does hold
from spring thru summer fall and cold
Creatures share this world we know
in all its wonder and its glow
reflecting back One eagles flight
soaring high and far from sight
seeing true one Gods true Gift
That eagle taught this soul to lift
Praise I will for all thats given
A book of life and names there written
where do creatures created fall
and Harken too they to a Call
In essence of where souls are sent
in time thru time our time is lent
One simple eagle gave cause my wonder
yet fearing not amidst loud thunder

One Song Sang Home
(November 10, 1978)

One day did bring one younger sort
with life to live and loves to cort
Not knowing well a love he found
though always feeling homesick bound

With style of voice one talent new
and all who heard his years were few
doors did open to his sound
while living life still homesick bound

A gift to take him high and far
and make him shine as to a star
his tone unique and now renown
yet all the years still homesick bound

When traveled down his waited road
Who had known what rivers flowed
His journey ends with somber sound
His life that left him
Homesick Bound

One Voice Was She—For Linda
(July 13, 2001)

Long ago and back in school
I knew one friend she was too cool
Though younger then she was no fool
Nor giving thoughts to one day rule

As aging to an adult she shined
With all that saw would fall behind
She held a gift so rare and kind
For me her gift to one day find

We spoke and kept in touch for years
We both became aware our fears
Too often too we shed our tears
Pain of life she still would clear

Now we both can see Mid age
we each still know and on each page
For me her friendship set the stage
One spirit free from guilded Cage

For now i see we made our choice
those years we had together few
For she had know i held a voice
Tho while I write she never knew

To be someone she hoped she'd be
This voice i held in Pen was She

One's Heart I knew
(January 24, 2010)

Whos gonna catch you before I do
Whos gonna lose out just on who
Who is gonna be left oh so blue
Be it me or be it you

The time it takes and pleasures sake
those reasons for be real or fake
your heart or mine or both at stake
and place one candle upon a cake

I see your eyes and seek to see
am I there to always be
set aside and far between
fortunes found yet money lean

thru it all we kept it burnin
for one another each and turnin
longin for and always yearn
a forest its floor with fragile fern

will you capture me before I you
who will be given or taken true
will skies be cloudy or always blue
Your heart keepin mine always knew

One's Heart One Found
(January 6, 2010)

I've looked and searched this country wide
to find to hold and belong to
One single soul he though did hide
among the shores and waters blue

always climbing walls so high
allow another enter in
With trust so clouded as the sky
Though yet not knowing who or when

In past this heart on shaking ground
and those that see are still forever blind
while silent voices lacking sound
and never knowing who to find

across so many bordered states
a longer journeys troubled road
when meeting many doubled fates
finding strength to share ones load

From texas to a southern State
did run across one singled out
where sunshine falls and never late
a single Man still having doubt

to yet instill a passion learned
A captured heart my own to be
those many bridges burned
does take to heart and always see
the One and only one for Me

One Single Gifted Love
(December 31, 2009)

being too far away,, and made to never stay
seeing through older eyes,, and hearing with leaner ears

recalling the kids at play,, and wheat in the fields that sway
having once touched the skies,, yet knowing let go the fears

walking with shorter steps,, and breathing a little faster
recalling in tears were wept..and seeing the doe in pasture

an earlier time in memory of,, and longing just to share
a Heart so full with Love,, yet finding no one to care

so often makes bitter a pill to take,, and fall upon lake waters still
for all who see for heavens sake,, who gains in love that will

to search the depths of sea and oceans,, and learn from fallen dreams
and finding not for true devotion,, a river fed of smaller streams

An ending comes from one begining,, and during all the while
a love with all thats missing,, just cant be done in style

to judge a gift wrapped so neatly, that holds a painted Bow
those feelings hide discreetly,, yet love must one day Flow

A Partnered Soul
(December 18, 2009)

A friend of mine walked past the other day
I yelled his way to see what he had to say
he turned as if to wonder why
then walked a bit closer with a heavy sigh
Well he said he had become a bit of a lost soul
and he needed to go off in search of it I was told
I pondered what he said and took a subtle step aside
I took his arm and calmy walked beside
How many days this been your feelin I asked
as we each walked a distance being tasked
This friend I have known for many a year
trying hard to shield and hide one hidden tear
asked did I ever know a partner be set in stone
as soldiers of a war give his life for only one
I told this friend of course and that I knew so well
this was the reason first i did his way yell
and that too a friend is more than just a treasured gift
For in the span of time and creation
There is no greater Lift a soul can reach and be swift
For I could see the soul he had lost and searching for was me
his soulmate, his partner, his friend, don't you see

47

One Partnered Test
(December 29, 2009)

A partner thru this life I'm told
tho often lost and often missed
should be as valued as pure gold
never measured or just one to list
A Soulmate always sought for true
As if ones Goal set to achieve
Never taken granted Few
Tho at times ones heart worn
one ones sleeve
While captured from a first hello
Knowing Not from happen stance
Two hearts combined and all aglow
can yet be viewed becomes a dance
For in where destiny leads us past
and fate steps in and sometimes test
Does love prevail and do outlast
The many trials and lay to rest
For one true partner once is found
had best be held and tightly kept
if ever lost nor hear one sound
as silent as tears often wept
This one best partner given me
and always walk beside and thru
Time passing marching onward see
To always Hold a soulmate True

A Path We Walk
(January 12, 2010)

People walk into our lives and seldom see a reason
then others step outside the path with every given season

To hold to thoughts awakened from one hidden frame of mind
to toss aside we often fail discover where to find

in pictures framed and portraits rare we feel we always hold
Those faces left inplace with care and rarely bought or sold

For memory sake and those that wake not holding to a dream
to cherrish loves and past hellos once found along a stream

Our lives we live and gifts we give to those we treasure most
In pride we keep and never weep yet seldom are the host

while By and By with labored sigh and troubles linger where
we reach so high to touch a sky, and blind in suns true glare

For many standing to our sides and those that cross our path
So few held near while some will hide some keep in bitter wrath

For many walking through our hearts and never leave one trace
Are those the few we tore apart and leave their tear stained face

Advice for many comes at cost and never truely heeded
Knowing One that walked beside was one i dearly needed

A Pattern Mystery
(December 21, 2009)

why are angel patterns seen
when kids lay flat
and pretend having wings

why are groups of geese always in the pattern V
as if to say just follow me

why do all one type of fish
known a pattern school
do they make one wish

So many tiny questions for
things so huge and that call
for herein see the pattern wonder
a wonder of it all

for me i see the signs
more often gone unseen
and with some i find
A strength on which to lean

For in this mystery all will seek
one answer for the fall
as winter turns a season peak
another year of patterns call
to mystery

A Poet Gift
(December 21, 2009)

In words I choose to phrase and write
and wonder where to place
Few words can ever mention
A love behind the Face

Ones eyes to be a window
in which to gaze upon
the spirit soul and essence
as sunlight steals the dawn

To never see a rainbows end
the gold that legends speak
Can there be a truer Friend
than one who's heart is meek

This life thus far has given
One path still oh so far and long
In each new day thats risen
what words did i choose wrong

A gift is often well too often taken
for less than truly be
something far more shakin
This Poet found in me

A Poet's Burden
(July 6, 2001)

Having thoughts with words to ryhme
to never know yet is there time
for placing in and of each line
what feelings share and bring to mind

Joining words with heart felt scheem
so often tall this task does seem
in nights with dreams a flowing stream
words descend from mystic beam

Some do say a poets gift
to touch the heart and soul to lift
tho in each line the love will shift
at times do spill through words i sift

All too well knowing to place in passion
and see what few these thoughts may fassion
to have a skill for love be certain
knowing well this poets burden

Race Of Years
(December 10, 2009)

Once in days past, who does the choosin to outlast the last
in runnin a race behind or in chase,
when in time and pick up the pace
faster and farther left many behind,
those up ahead I look to and find
while life is a race though often is seen
trials and lessons throughout which we gleen
Many a turns and twists in the road
knowing never we are headed where rivers once flowed
too often encumbered and yielding in truth
and look to our past and long for our youth
at times must we envy those lesser in years
accepting ourselves and dry our own tears
For Not having Loved but once given the chance
mistaken our path yet seen at one glance
Where we are now and where have we been
this Race our lives given a breath in the end

Regain The Heart
(July 1, 2010)

people pass into our lives
and come to clear the clouds away
they make so blue our bluer skies
yet never seem to stay
We all are like one sandy beach
with many tides that touch
some come to learn and some to teach
with some who give so much

seldom kept a length of time
once touched and held so close
some songs contain a bitter rhyme
as fragrant as the rose

For Some a talent hidden true
take lifetimes to discover
as hearts are shared yet oh so few
this test we test each other
From the corners of creation
with winds that often voice
in life we hold one station
Nor given to by choice

with convictions true and standards high
never bending straight and through
with passions such that touch the sky
this Me I am you never knew
For in these lines so written here
I hope one may discover
was You who held me near and fear
our hearts we each recover

River Of Friendship
(June 12, 1993)

Always through life we look and we hope
Not to loose grip or fall from lifes rope
Reaching for others tho loose them we will
Having been lost and how to refill
Some will they find as trying to show
How to maintain and not to let go
Our lives are as rivers some never to flow
With deeds of our fathers and seeds we will sew
Knowin though once my life I did cross
Those blessings I counted and gifts I did toss
what some had become and fail yet to be
No others yet known So few to yet see
My thoughts going back gives note to another
The friends I do have with some as no other
Friends do become with reasons unseen
Some washed in the blood and still be unclean
This friend I had found with heart and with mind
Time keeps us apart and change cannot find
So near are the signs ones end is to come
See now what one missed nor cared of by some
Suffer will one to seek and discover
Assessed by redemption though yet to uncover
One must remain the other must go
One life at an end
Ones river to flow

Room Of Eternity
(December 11, 2009)

No Truer Heart has ever known
For heavens Sake and do atone
Do Gods on high deliver seasons
That pass with time to give us reason
A Youth once held tho often wasted
As wine thats aged and still untasted
Will Mankind and all his wonder
Search the tides hear oceans thunder
Revealing Not no answers clear
While always ponder Fate draws Near
To Seek in silence voiced on high
Are Gods so distant do they Sigh
Trouble not the Spirits will
Calling out with Hearts that spill
Overwhelming All that Hear
A second coming yields its fear
Be we alone or fall together
in summers calm or stormy weather
Upon one highway straight and narrow
God cradle close a fallen sparrow
While in this light until rainbows end
forever and always we pray to spend
Where Gods have spared our souls their place
Among this Vast and awesome space

A Sailor's Sonnet
(May 12, 1993)

Ships at sea and breakers to sunder
clouds that gather yielding loud thunder
sailors were lost round capes did explore
their ships did they master with sail rigging tore
while steady on course deep waters did yearn
the albatros' flight to port and astern
many afar away coasts they did seek
while mastering crafts round death daring reef
billowing sails and pillowing clouds
mighty the whale and dolphins in crowd
No shore is too distant that break away tide
An ocean so Vast yet nowhere to hide
searching to answer this call from the sea
those ships tossed by the waves and tempting to flee
Old boats of the past unlike those today
Down were they cast and long are to stay
In hearts and in mind are legends they say
A Sailor of salt,,tho still made of clay

Seasons Fold
(September 11, 2010)

Let me be the seed you Sew to make your
lawn so green to show
i want to be your summer rain
to ease the Heat that cause
you pain
In fall i hope to be your rake
to gather leaves for winters sake
Let me be your snowplow when
snow does fall
and keep your path clear
for spring to call
the Seasons come and go so fast
and leave us looking to the past
for time that measures what it will
with hearts that falter others fill
This Calendar of Life
with measured strife
With Seasons fold one
to another
each year tho passes
seen by Natures Mother

Sidelines Of A Tear
(March 28, 2010)

sittin on the sidelines knowin
your one of those rare finds
does it do me any good
for all intents and purpose
makin me just wanna curse
and still luvin you as I should
always willin and always givin
never true for myself or my own true livin
Still holdin on as the bark to the wood
See when ya come along and spoke one sound
in your voice and in one you found
the one thing best in life you stood
in all the years waitn and all the years chasin
for me to know deep it's you I'd be a facin
tellin me to wait as if ya knew I could
Weeks goin by and into months I'm here
still sittin on the sidelines now still it's clear
ya stole this heart as tho ya knew you should
shoulda woulda coulda kept from me
coulda shouldya would ya ever see
did I wear a sign saying vacancy the
hearts we joined now in ecstasy

So Into You
(March 20, 2010)

Well here is a little something
Ii thought you need to know
just why or when or how
the one that sets your heart and passions glow
too often led away and taken at surprise
the one ya wish could always say they'd stay
and glanced at with your eyes
i hope to feel your touch and wanted for so long
these things we want so much in life
like rhyme to each and every song
this little somethin held for you
in time that I could share
the reasons why my sky is blue
and carry Love to where
and keep you safe in knowing
sharing all we never knew
for sake of love and friendship and just be kept together
knowing each this day us two a little better
to lose to win or draw and never cross the line
nobody suits me more and you are Oh so fine
So here ive said it here that one thing you should know
one little thing to share and be allowed to show
Now whats the plan to play or pass
or take it slow or take it fast
All I know is im where I want to be
me with you and you with me
nothing needs to change or alter til' we step
my heart with yours and yours with mine
and be they always kept

One Star Of Fate
(July 20, 2010)

Wherever you are, whatever you do
far from your star, my lite is for you
at times lost and alone, and feeling too blue
this carved into stone, tho never you knew
One bound tho kept far, the other still fear
each heart with one scar, yet healed by
one tear
Some being shallow, and few that are deep
you minded I'd follow, in faith still to leap
throughout all seasons, and always in time
for whatever reasons, the hours that chime
why did you come to be, if not just for me
never to part, and willing to see
these years passing fast, as blue as the sea
let go of the past, and stand only with me
The Star you are from, your light it will shine
For me you had come, and stay for all time
Was Fate the soul purpose
Or one destiny still mine

Stetsons Two
(February 5, 2010)

Stetsons meet and yet may walk
in boots with spurs that seem to talk
side by side as partners meant
ones total heart the other spent
one lifes journey long yet true
the others way be somber and blue
when happen to see if not per chance
did fate play along to lend one glance
one meant to gaurd from harm and keep
the others trust with faith to leap
to keep a balance and union there
their thoughts and past to always share
be committed and lasting true
forsaken shaken of devotion too
for herein lies the bond to bind
one sighted seen and yet been blind
one stetson to stetson in all does contain
one for the other as constant as rain
to walk one path and not to fall
a solid partner to answer one call
in stetsons with wranglers faded blue
and Boots with spurs that spoke for who
this one tall cowboy I long for true
I tips my Hat to One who's you

Stolen Heart
(February 27, 2010)

there are at times things come to mind
where hearts just never mend
and always free and meant to me
my own for who to send
some are given some are taken
some are often stole
but this one lingers on alone
and never finds its role
For many years with many tears
and still unknown for Size
This passion and its love for all
yet never seen through clearer eyes
Still yet willing and so tempted
test those hands of fate
and always see and still yet free
this one forsaken late
Bitter rigid cold and worn
as sails blown far at sea
this heart in me and with it born
will and still and never be
ever stole from me

Stranger Am I
(June 20, 1990)

The Moment I saw your face at my door
I wondered would I see and hear more
Your eyes gave clue to stories untold
As found with Surprise the secrets you hold
Those things you did share with me on that day
Your voice so distinct and held me at bay
I thought in my mind to catch in mid air
Your heart thrown to me you saw I could care
My Home is now yours the door you did close
behind you with ease your fear still arose
I calmed your concern with concern of my own
For you were unlike no other I had known
I looked out to see One Star in the Sky
That one I had noticed you held in your eye
Though still I'm alone for you had passed by
One heart of a stranger, one stranger am I

Who Sweeps The Night
(December 09, 2009)

An Angel sits upon the Moon
who sweeps the starlite dusk til noon
while wonder how and just for whom
Those yielding hearts of spacious room
Given passion comes of late
and taken far handpicked by fate
to those of patience long and wait
resistance peaks where time abate
For Some so true and thought so pure
Do treasure one and be we sure
A spirit ill yet strives to cure
and self assurance be secure
When look on high to heavens gold
scattered trails all to unfold
Is hidden there by ages old
Amidst the timeless measures told
One Angels Task the Heavens Hold

A Switch Of My Heart
(May 31, 2010)

Someone comes along tho you never know to say
just what it is to care or carry on that way
they make you fly as high as eagles far aloft
why did you turn me on, then choose to turn me off

Why did you lite this fire and cause this heart to yearn
why have you come along to only let it burn
i held you in my dreams yet missing you it seems
why did you turn me on and have my passions steam

you crossed my trail so sudden an yet with breaking speed
you told me all the things that you knew alone id heed
and when attached I grew you swore ya never knew
why have you turned me on now like a bird you flew

Why do you turn me on and inside out as well
a heart so full for one you shattered quick the shell
for growin close tho seemed to not be far removed
why did you turn me on igniting flames ensued

So turn me off and keep your distance far from me
you played my heart as if a banjo on yur knee
that longing for your love has turned now bitter sweet
why did you turn me on to leave me in bare feet

Why did you turn me on with words and caution of
the love that ony two compared with lasting love
So march on down your path and seek just one more heart
for one day soon will be your own you break apart

Taken Dreams
(December 7, 2009)

I dreamed a dream of silence which stood apart
a crowd of wonder and amazement of heart
I sought a place to stand alone yet never knowing true
tho ponder long a trust i knew
This depth of spirit that becons all
While in seclusion takes the fall
Regaining will and strength to stand
who will come forth to take my hand
I walked a Path so few have known
yet never have I stood alone
For in a crowded Sea of souls
amidst endeavors we find our goals
My own has been to capture still
a soulmates heart that I can fill
When years have passed and know they Do
this Heart I'll give to One thought True
In Time the essence ages on
To Dream the dreams of those now gone

Taken Hearts
(January 29, 2010)

Where in one life do we find one start
so many roads and tracks to chart
sometimes together and often apart
just let em hear the beat of your heart

To wonder along and follow thru
still knowin things yet never knew
counting loves some 2 by 2
dont let em see your heart so blue

holdin on with knuckles white
struggle long and win the fight
who was wrong and was I right
dont let em lose your heart from sight

clouds that gather will often rain
does no one see or feel ones pain
just as able was brother cain
dont let em steal your heart for gain

when fallin far and falling true
who still suffers most for who
only know and walk in my shoe
DO let em have my heart they knew

Taken Voyage
(June 28, 2001)

One night amidst the stillness peace
I dreamed of leaving space
to go beyond and never cease
in flight as though to race
I traveled far and oh so long
though feeling not the pain
as far ahead to hear a song
and keeping in the lane
This seemed to be a better task
for with me there was you
and all the while I dared to ask
Why were the stars so few
I reached the shore and there you stood
you knew my heart was shaken
to find you here as if I could
with fears of loss to awaken
all from this voyage
once taken

A Hidden Dream
(December 8, 2009)

I often find you at my side
I also see you run and hide
why wont you hang around and see
or are you just afraid of me
I offer nothing more from me
than all there is that you can see
your touch your voice is something rare
why wont you see that I do care
in dreams we walk and freely share
each others thoughts and whispers there
then waken to this vacancy
this space you filled in slumber flee
I find you close and yet so far
as if I try to grasp a star
One day I long for yours and mine
our hearts and soul to intertwine
in only dreams you still abide
from there I see in you I hide

The Want To
(April 5, 2010)

For those who just yet will not see
there is a forrest with just one tree
why did you do it why cant ya be
ya done took the want to outta me
With days that fold on into weeks
and me the one ya told did seek
and dance weve done as cheek to cheek
this one true heart here oh so meek
you said ya never knew it tho ya
seemed to get on through it
a feelin lost ya threw away
but still im here and always stay
So why cant ya see
that forrest for a tree took for granted three
done took the want to outta me
yeh ya took that want to outta me
strike one, strike two and now number 3
ya had a chance to hold on to me
i done lost the want to dont ya see
one desire no longer fair
and once ya held to me with care
now off in distance you now do stare
a bitter feelin now i bare
Now with the want no longer there

Think Of Me
(February 24, 2010)

*Who is out there to see me
how long will it take somone to be
that one most special meant just to see
the real who I am the me in me*

*the mileage we endure and always sustain
is constant as always a summer rain
reflected at times with Hearts in pain
to keep things together and keep in one lane*

*that highway of life with twist and with turn
a fire to remains always and always will burn
as winds of a storm as thoughts I have churn
for all in this life we seldom do learn*

*Be tested and tried and given to change
Broad are our views tho Narrow yet strange
To ever still pass my way or in range
to often upset or let rearrange*

*Ones thinking of life and all can attain
We step on some hearts and do inflict pain
whose face did we see one tear tho did stain
and also with cause and always regain*

*this me i do know and me i will be
while others look on and never will see
as a forrest has so many began with one tree
with my thoughts too are many belonging to me*

Time To Be Worth
(December 7, 1987)

The wheel of time if made to yield
our lives were cast with souls be sealed
where may we find a path to tred
how many will search and who will be led
The Spring of eternity show life its one course
A summer of existence one world as in force
Time of itself we known to be free
Search for and found a future to see
Though as we yet linger we wonder and wait
with Loves we did find in dreams that were late
Know we no reason or to question why
Still are we here and still we yet Sigh
As we will enter lifes Season of fall
Silence was broken a world had one call
As winters abound with blankets of cold
our souls crying out as of to be gold
In time to be worth in time are we sold

Time To Fade
(July 5, 1989)

Time is said to fly
Time is said we're given to die
Time is all to often less
Time to measure ones success

Time will cause a wound to grow
Time will also Heal we know
Time itself does never hide
Time is the wheel on which we ride

Time will buffer anxious thought
Time to suffer lessons taught
Time for all to reap and Sew
Time to Learn with Time to know

Time for Young and time for old
Time for warmth and time for cold
Time for shelter in the shade
When will Time begin to fade

Time That Mends
(January 17, 2010)

I will mend in time this heart of mine
and come back around to stand in line
See the distance that I can go
and take a better breather tho still wont know

How far to go and find one trace
Who travels fast but loose the race
an end in sight tho head full steam
does it all stand apart yet left unseen

Having walked run and driven one long winding road
Yet wonder who has eyes for who had glowed
in lifes fuller measure on to our ends
Time alone is always the the thing that mends

For give our hearts to many with one it stays
a never ending story and on stage one plays
to capture and conceal in ones betterment of
something took for granted tho gives full Love

To mend a shattered dream leaves some to know
tho when a heart is broked and beating slow
and try and find the pieces scattered all around
and wonder still will stand on solid ground

In knowing comes repair of hearts that share
one and to another with eyes that stare
When given free to others is seldom known
A mended Heart is stronger with radiance shown

Twice In Pain
(December 12, 1983)

Are we really over one another
does the lighting come before the thunder
should our road in life just fall assunder
will what we shared be kept in wonder
With arms around my soul and heart
did warm the spirit as tho fine art
this path we chose could no one chart
Why has time caused us to part
This love for you could be so bold
Without a love do we grow cold
The good in life is rare im told
So will I see before I'm old
Some loves are found as at a glance
A second Love be left to chance
When Love was young the two would dance
As twice in Pain from Lovers Lance

Two Test
(April 4, 2010)

I thought we were always meant for one true purpose in life
Boys grow into men and some do take a wife
With lives for some are wreckless and blue
and some with Years of struggles and strife
There be one and only constant that never ends
just as any river follows one course with many bends
Ending To a larger home where few seldom holds
just as a truer love with undending love one sends
given said for a picture to hold a thousand words and yet
I took a stand and long the cost and still did bet
a wager for a treasure unknown
nor judge no one from once had grown
A better feeling closer grown closer to
and seperate so many from few
did wear a crease of lines and tear
that last now deeper throught out one year
to trust and offer up ones will
what comes of age and and with that still
no hands of fate will hold or lend
a test of time that has no end

View Of Mind
(November 9, 1987)

Today I feel as though to see
A window Cast my world it be
Alone i stare at life and dream
With clouds that roll with thunder scream
Though far away in mind im gone
Green the fields of grass and lawn
To catch a Whisper hold me still
ones eyes with tears do often fill
Still Wonder I with thoughts of you
A mirror I find who looks to Who
Amidst the breaking tides of time
One Bell to ring one day and chime
Far I see myself I fear
Was life of Love so Far so Near
A window darkens Dusk and wait
A Heart and Soul had seen too late
I still yet gaze through windows pane
though darker now with more refrain
While constant as a summer Rain
In View of Mind a Windows Pain

Who's Heart Have You Known
(January 16, 2010)

Who ya gonna have and who will be one knowin
The heart you've held inside keeps on beatin and aglowin
If taken by the hand and led to walk away
tho all the while your wishin just to want to stay

In silence and in noise there is one truth kept deep
A heart tho scarred and shaken with faith do we still leap
the many and the few bestowed of greater gifts
ones heart of truer passion and spirit only lifts

Whos heart is this your knowin, with seeds of kindness showin
the trails and roads forsaken and summer breeze be blowin
to walk anothers life, you step inside their shoes
to know about their strife and feel and know their blues

To walk beside and linger, a burden thought to share
and often times a stranger will also show can care
is said to hold and trust, good deeds come back around
as men are made of dust and oneday enter ground

In life our hearts are taken, and some are clearly stole
while some are also fakin and who does share the role
the one heart youve been knowin, for granted cannot fall
a shield around it high, to climb a splintered wall

This ones heart youve been knowin and gaze with eyes now dim
the many chances taken and many chances slim
This one heart keeps on beatin and love inside glows on
those many trials defeatin and still can hear the song

So whos heart you been knowin
and wonder far and wide
My own Heart still is flowin
A deeper love inside